I0546532

L.A.
MUMMY

LANCE LOOT

D & T
PUBLISHING

This one's for the real Bark Mouglas, the kookiest dude this side of the Pacific!

"L.A. Woman, L.A. Woman,

L.A. Woman, you're my woman!"

— *"L.A. Woman"* by The Doors

"Know this: this creature is the bringer of death. He

will never eat, he will never sleep, and he will never

stop."

— *The Mummy*, 1999 film

L.A.

MUMMY

CHAPTER ONE

THE PHOENIX RISING FROM THE STEAMING PILE OF SHIT

A fresh start.

That's exactly what I needed and was looking for when I moved to Galena—one of those old-ass port cities for those not familiar—early last fall.

My name is Bark Mouglas and I'm thirty-four years young. Because, ya know, thirties are the new twenties and all that.

I had to do a stint in rehab—ex-alkie here at your service, and believe me, the shit that happened in rehab would make for a crazy book itself... ask me some other time about The Wizard—and I recently earned my ninety-day sobriety chip. That was a really big deal for me because in the height of my addiction, I couldn't get through a day without a fifth of Jack.

Anyway, this hotel out in Galena offered me a job in charge of running sound for big events, and I saw it as the perfect opportunity to start over, kinda like a phoenix rising out of a steaming pile of shit.

Yeah, I'm a techie guy; got my degree from Columbia in audio engineering and have never looked back since. Except when I was searching for the bottom of a bottle, but that's all in the past now.

My first couple days in Galena went well. Learned the ropes at the hotel and moved into my new digs. My apartment is on the second floor—accessible on the outside by this wooden stairway/balcony combo—and it's pretty spacious and nice. However, my landlord Dale is a fat drunken asshole. In fact, he makes me back in my worst days look like a Disney princess on ice, and that's saying a lot. The second night there, I finally got all my shit unpacked and situated, when I heard this heavy lumbering outside my door. Then, someone on the other side jammed a key in the lock— took them a few tries, too—unlocking, and opening the door.

And Dale's rotund form was swaying in the doorway, and I could tell the guy was completely three dumbass sheets to the wind. He scared me at first, too. Like what the hell, man, this is my place, I don't care if you're the landlord, it's almost freaking midnight. Ya don't come barging into a dude's apartment like that.

"Dale, what the hell are you doing here?" I asked.

He stumbled into the room.

"Those… those *bastards*! Down on the floor

below ya… they ain't payin' their *rent*! And… and ya gotta help me, you know… rough 'em up a bit!"

This guy gives drinkers a bad rap.

"Dale, you gotta go, man. You can't just stroll in here whenever you feel like it! And you freaked me out, too. You're lucky I didn't have my bow handy, cuz I wouldn't have hesitated making you shish kabob."

Just the thought of him roasting on a skewer—or arrow in this case—actually made me wanna vomit. And yeah, I took up archery after getting sober. Helps me release a lot of those dark thoughts, ya know?

Dale waddled forward and got right in my face, so close that the booze stench was overpowering. If I would have lit a match at that moment, his beach ball body would have instantly gone up in flames.

"You… you better pay *your* rent on time, buddy!" Dale said, his breath toxic. "Or we gonna have problems! You got that, Blart?"

I shook my head.

Awesome start, right?

"It's *Bark*, Dale. And I already paid my first month's rent with the security deposit. Obviously, you don't remember that."

Dale made an O with his mouth and started blinking a lot, like his one remaining brain cell was working overtime.

Something must have clicked, though, because then he nodded, did an about-face, and wobbled to the door.

"Okay, I'll be back later… to keep ya on your toes!" Dale slurred. "Have a good one!"

I closed the door behind him and made a mental note to install one of those chain things on the door. That'll keep him out, master key or no master key.

CHAPTER TWO

THAT'S ONE FREAKY SONOFABITCH

The rest of my first week in Galena was uneventful until the weekend hit, and on my birthday, specifically. So in the downtown area, I found this monster set of old concrete stairs that led to an upper area of the town where the fancier houses were at. For context, one of my favorite films is *Joker* with Joaquin Phoenix, and the first thing I pictured when I saw those stairs was the Joker dancing around like a kid in a candy store on them; they looked nearly identical to the ones used in the movie.

So for my birthday, after moving to a whole new city, surviving my first work week, and enduring all of dumbass Dale's bullshit, I was gonna recreate the iconic weirdo waltz and perform my very own *Joker* dance on these stairs. I even had my big noise-canceling headphones with '*The Hey Song*' queued up on my phone—and yes, I know it's truly titled '*Rock and Roll Part 2,*' but it's actually '*The Hey Song*' in spirit, so get with the times already if you're questioning me.

I'd practiced the moves plenty of times in the mirror before, so as the music rumbled and the *'HEYs'* entered the sonic fray, it didn't take long at all for me to get into the groove and lose myself in the *Joker* dance. The closest thing I can compare it to would be like a euphoric, meditative state of mind.

As the song began to fade out, I imagined that powerful stance the Joker is doing on the movie poster—you know the one—where he's on the stairs leaning back slightly with his arms out and his fists clenched, like he's just conquered the world. I closed my eyes and did that very same pose, even after the song had faded out entirely.

And as I held that pose, I felt really good, ya know? I really felt like I'd made it, like I finally did something right. I was able to get a hold on my demons and quit drinking, and now I had this whole fresh new world in front of me; new city, new job, new apartment, and it was all really empowering. Took me long enough to figure shit out, but better late than never, right?

Feeling on freaking cloud nine, I slowly opened my eyes to see this wrestler-looking guy and who I would assume to be his girlfriend near the bottom of the stairs, gawking at me. She was frowning and saying something, but I couldn't hear what, like a colorized silent film.

Then I remembered I had the noise-canceling headphones on. Still holding my power stance, I yanked the headphones off and draped them around my neck.

"Sorry, what'd ya say?" I asked.

She sighed, like I was asking her to lick a porcupine or something.

"I *said*," she replied, making sure to draw out the last word into two syllables. "What the hell are you doing? Is that supposed to be like a *Joker* pose or something?"

She may be a little aggressive, but at least she had good taste.

"Nah, it's a *Rocky* pose!" I replied sarcastically.

The wrestler-boyfriend came forward, staring daggers at me, and for whatever reason he looked mad as all hell.

"Yo, did you just call my girl a cocky bimbo, bro?!"

The mood officially murdered, I relaxed and abandoned the *Joker* stance.

"No, man! I was joking, I just said I was doing a *Rocky* pose. Ya know, like—"

"Yo shut up, bro! I'm gonna come up there and stuff those headphones in your—"

What happened next will be forever branded into my brain. Before he could finish his threat, the wrestler-boyfriend was interrupted by this... *thing*—I think it was male, though?—that emerged from the shadows behind a nearby building; it shrieked in what I can only describe as a high-pitched death-metal scream, but like it was doing it with an inhaling technique.

"L.A. MUMMY!" the thing shrieked.

To me, it sounded like the thing was trying to match the same melody Jim Morrison sang when he belted the title phrase in The Doors song *'L.A. Woman,'* but with those death-metal vocals, who the hell knows for sure.

So this thing, guy, whatever—hell, I'm just gonna start calling it the L.A. Mummy—had this enormous green afro that was the size of an exercise ball (it *had* to be fake), these dirty purple samurai-style pants, and its entire torso was wrapped with the filthiest gauze I've ever seen. I don't wanna know what those bandages were caked and smeared with, but it was likely a potluck of the foulest substances imaginable. The skin on its face and arms was pasty, slightly jaundiced even.

I remember my first thought was, *this dude cannot be fucking real.*

The wrestler-boyfriend, seeing the L.A. Mummy, yelped and jumped back in fright, his face turning pure white. The girlfriend grabbed Mr. Big Tough Guy's arm and pulled him so they could continue down the sidewalk; he was still looking at the L.A. Mummy, all spooked, and his expression was like he had just seen the living dead. All show, no go.

The girlfriend looked at the L.A. Mummy, then to me on the stairs.

"Yeah, that's some real nice company you keep there… fuckin' *freaks!*"

And they trudged off.

I looked at the L.A. Mummy—who was now staring at me, and I came to the horrible realization that it had probably watched me the whole time I was doing my *Joker* dance—and felt a sickening sensation in my stomach that I was actually being associated with this freaky sonofabitch!

"Hey, I don't know him!" I called after the couple, but I'm sure they were too far to hear me.

The L.A. Mummy was doing an excited wheeze-giggle. I could tell this dude had taken five or six too many rides on the weird wagon, and I needed to get the hell outta Dodge. I descended the stairs, but when I got to the bottom, we locked eyes.

"Yeah, uhh…" I said, unsure of what to say. "You definitely look like a *Joker* fan too, so… place is all yours! Have at it!"

"*L.A. MUMMY!*"

I had seen and heard more than enough. I freaking booked it home.

C H A P T E R   T H R E E

T H E   V I N N Y   V A N U C C H I ' S   F I A S C O

That night, I don't know why, but I had a bad feeling that creeper was gonna decide to pay me a visit. And I was freaking the hell out because of it. Just something about that guy, that *thing*… the dude was definitely half a bubble off plumb, and I'd even say giving him the benefit of a half bubble was a stretch.

I'd be lying if I said I didn't hear any odd noises that night. I heard some scurrying and scratching outside on the balcony, but I would say that could have been attributed to some coked-out varmint. Hey, cocaine-fueled rat fights are a real thing. I wish I was making that up, but I'm not. I also wish I could say I've never attended and/or bet on one, but I have. Regardless, I did not hear that maniac wail his hellish rendition of '*L.A. Woman*' once the whole night, so I took that as a win.

The next week progressed swimmingly. Work was

pie, Dale mostly left me alone, and I didn't catch a single glimpse of that L.A. Mummy. Also, there was this really cute waitress, Jessica, at this old-school Italian joint I had started frequenting called Vinnie Vanucchi's.

I probably had had Jessica as a server three times or so and we always had decent conversation, definitely seemed like there was some chemistry there, ya know? So this time, I was gonna crank up the ol' Mouglas charm to eleven and ask her out on a real date. I didn't own any super fancy threads, so the best I could do was wear a snazzy gray blazer over my Nintendo 64 T-shirt.

I got seated at a corner table against a big window, giving me a nice view of the river. The place seemed dead, so I was hoping that would give Jessica and I an opportunity to talk more.

"Well, hello there!" Jessica said, gliding to my table.

"Hey, what's up?" I replied.

"So, what're you having on this fine afternoon?"

"Angel hair pasta al dente with pig trotter sauce… and a Pepsi, please."

"Ahh, opting for the usual go-to then, huh?"

"Absolutely, it's always freaking delicious."

I was trying really hard to think of a way to steer the exchange toward asking her out without seeming like a weirdo, but man, I was shootin' blanks. I'd been outta the game for way too long.

"I'll put that order in and be right back with your drink!"

Before I could pull something witty to say out of my ass, she was off. Strike one for me. So much for that ol' Mouglas charm.

I started to brainstorm potential conversation topics when I saw Jessica coming back with my soda. Alright, game on.

She set my drink in front of me.

"Your food should be coming out shortly."

"Yeah, thanks! So, uhh… what's new? Anything?"

"Oh, nothing much! Same old, same old. Working here, my cats, 'bout it really!"

"Ahh, that's right! I remember you telling me about your cats. Three of 'em, right? Tuxedo, Baxter, and… uhh… Zero! … I think!"

She laughed, which thankfully meant I was doing something right.

"Wow, good memory! Yup, they're my furry little babies! Oh, I think I see your food on the counter. Let me grab it and then I'll show you obligatory cat pics!"

She went off to snag my food. I leaned back in my chair and smiled; this seemed to be going far better than I had expected. Those cat pics were sure to get my foot in the door now.

She returned with my plate of noodles. I freaking love it when food is so hot you can see the wispy little tendrils of steam, because when you take that first bite, damn does it burn. And that food burn is about the closest and safest way I can get to reliving the abrasive feeling of whiskey blazing down my throat. I'd be lying if I said I didn't miss it sometimes.

"Angel hair pasta al dente with pig trotter sauce," Jessica announced, placing the food in front of me. "And be careful, that plate is really hot!"

Without wasting a single moment, I dug into the noodles and shoveled a gob right into my mouth. The burn was instantaneous, and I relished in it as I felt the scorching mass steadily navigate its way to my stomach.

"Oh, my," Jessica said. "Pretty hungry there, huh? Haha!"

I gobbled another bite in before replying. And damn, those pig trotters really made that sauce culinary heaven.

"Just a wee bit. God, I swear… this keeps getting better every time!"

She smiled.

"That's great! Really happy to hear that. I'll be sure to pass it on to the cooks!"

I swallowed my mouthful.

"So how 'bout them cat pics, eh? I'd love to see the furry rascals, I'm a fellow cat-lover myself."

Her face lit up like a movie-theater marquee.

"Oh, of *course*! Here, let me pull some up…"

Jessica leaned over with her phone and scrolled

through her gallery. I kid you not, there must have been hundreds of pics of these felines. Cute little things, but damn, guess she wasn't messing around when she called 'em her babies.

I 'awww'd and 'ooo'd and 'wow'd at all the appropriate moments, and I could tell it was making her happy. And if I'm being honest, seeing Jessica smile and get all animated about her cats, well, it made me happy, too. It also made me feel like a connection was formed between us, and I finally built up the nerve to ask the big question and bring it all home.

"So Jessica, I was wondering… how would you like it if you and I… well, if you and I—"

I was interrupted by Jessica's loud, banshee-like scream. And she scared me, too. I almost fell right out of my chair. I looked at her and noticed her staring at something behind me with wide-eyed horror. So I spun around to see what had gotten her screaming like she was being chased by Leatherface, and… wow. At first, I felt like my heart skipped a couple beats, but then I just felt rage. Like, Incredible Hulk level of rage, too.

The L.A. Mummy had its hideous face, specifically the massive blistered lips of its open mouth, smushed up against the window. And it kept rubbing its vile purple tongue along the glass, getting spit and some slimy substance everywhere.

"*L.A. MUMMY!*" it shrieked—try repeating that phrase while holding your tongue to get an idea how it sounded exactly.

Incensed beyond belief, I locked eyes with the L.A. Mummy. If looks could kill, this freaky asshole would be dismembered into dime-sized bits, thereby cast into the fires of Mt. Doom.

"You again?!" I yelled at the thing. "What the hell are you doing here?! And *stop licking the freaking window, that's disgusting!*"

Of course, me saying that just made it lick the glass with even more gusto. This had gone too far now. I was ready to kick its dirty mummy ass all the way to next Sunday. I was gonna—

"You *know* this sicko?!" Jessica exclaimed.

Alarmed, I wheeled to face her. No way in hell was I going to let someone else associate me with this abomination!

"*No*! No, I don't! But I think it might be following me! You see… last week, over on those big concrete stairs downtown, I was doing the *Joker* dance—"

"You think this is *funny*?!" she interrupted. "Like some kind of stupid prank? Because I'm not laughing!"

She went to leave.

"NO! Wait, Jessica!"

She twirled and looked at the L.A. Mummy, still licking the glass, and then at me, her face scowling in disgust.

"You're both *sick*. Don't ever come here again, you understand? Please."

Then she left the room and disappeared. And I immediately felt like total hot garbage. Like I shrank into the smallest man in the world. It wasn't fair, everything had been going so well. We had been chatting it up, establishing a connection, and then…

That filthy bastard.

White-hot anger surged through me and I rushed to the window, my face and the L.A. Mummy's separated only by the paper-thin pane of glass.

"You mummy sonofabitch, you're ruining *everything* for me, do you realize that?!" I bellowed. "I came here to get a fresh start, a new beginning! Shed my old skin! And *you won't let me*! I've practically been to the goddamn grave and back, and I just wanna finally have a normal life for once! Okay? *So leave me the fuck alone*!"

I punched the glass as hard as I could and it made a dull thud. The L.A. Mummy didn't even flinch, but it un-smushed its face from the window and smiled. Its stupid green afro jiggled as it moved. I think I only counted four teeth in its hellacious crater of a mouth, but they were all canines, big and razor sharp, too.

"*L.A. MUMMY!*"

Pissed off to the max, I punched the window again and immediately wished I hadn't, because damn did that freaking hurt. I got up and left Vinnie Vanucchi's, probably for the last time because I knew I wasn't gonna be welcomed back after that shitshow.

My hand was throbbing, and I rubbed it as I plodded down the sidewalk in the direction of my apartment. I wished it could have been aching from caving that lunatic's face in instead of thumping a window. At the very least, why couldn't the glass have shattered or something cool? Then I could have wrung that L.A. Mummy's chicken neck afterwards, too.

I looked over my shoulder, half-expecting to see those billowy samurai pants and bobbing green afro behind me, but thankfully, no freakshows in sight. Probably off ruining someone else's life. I traipsed along and let my overactive mind wander, trying to think of something else for a change. I decided to call up my friend.

Larry, my buddy from back home—I need to stop saying it like that because *this*, Galena, is my home now—was planning to come up and check out my place later this week. And man, could I use a familiar face… or I guess familiar *voice* in this regard. He picked up on the second or third ring.

"Hey, how's it going, Bark?" Larry said through the phone.

"Larry! Good to hear your voice! And I've been better, dude… definitely been better. On top of all that shit I was telling you about with my landlord, I think I got myself a damn stalker now, too."

"Umm… come again? A stalker… *really*? Man or woman?"

"I think man, but I'm not a hundred percent sure on that. It seems to only ever say *'L.A. Mummy'* so… that's its name to me. Sort of like a nightmarish Pokémon I guess. Plus, it's wrapped up in these dirty-ass bandages and it has a big green afro."

"…*what*?! And you're saying this thing is *stalking* you?! That's messed up! I mean, I was planning on leaving tomorrow to head up by you, but do you think it's safe for me to come? This all sounds like a shitty horror movie or something, dude."

"No, it's safe here, man! The L.A. Mummy seems harmless in a physical sense… it hasn't laid a finger on me or anything, it's just destructive as all hell when it comes to butting into my life."

"Bark, don't screw around with this! Just because it hasn't done anything really bad yet doesn't mean it won't! Get your ass to the police station and file a restraining order against this… mummy, freak, whatever it is!"

"Huh… that's actually a damn good idea, Larry. I hadn't even thought of that."

"Yeah, well take the damn good idea and run with it! Please, for your sake *and* mine. Because when I get there, I really don't want to be followed everywhere by some mummy maniac, okay?"

"Yeah… you know what, Larry? I'm actually gonna go to the police station right now. This L.A. Mummy can go scratch a cactus, it's done enough damage. Thanks again, dude."

"Not a problem. I'll let you know when I'm leaving tomorrow. See ya soon, man! And good luck!"

I hung up and instantly felt better about everything. Now I had a viable solution that would hold some water. I gotta hand it to Larry, he was golden for that. I changed course and headed for the police station. I was going to file a restraining order against that invasive L.A. Mummy, and that was that. If it didn't want to honor the order and still tried to make my life hell, go right ahead—that'll grant you residency in the pokey, ya wannabe Tut. Lock that cell and toss the freaking key into the Dead Sea.

C H A P T E R   F O U R

D E P U T Y   D A W G S

I strode into the police station like a man with a plan and full of promise. The surly officer at the front desk had a hefty handlebar mustache and definitely fit the bill of being someone's weird uncle. I noisily cleared my throat to get the guy's attention. He didn't seem to be doing a whole hell of a lot, yet he acted like looking up from his papers to acknowledge my presence was worse than getting a tooth pulled.

"Help you?" he grumbled.

"Yeah, hi… so who do I talk to around here about filing a restraining order against someone? It's pretty important, I think I have a stalker."

Mr. Handlebar 'Stache rolled his eyes and let out a mammoth sigh. He turned his head to face behind him.

"*Aimaro*!" he barked, kinda sounding like Oscar the Grouch. "Get your ass over here! Got a guy who says he's got a stalker situation. Help him out, will ya?"

He looked back at me and chuckled.

"Nice blazer/T-shirt combo," Handlebar said sarcastically. "Hot date or somethin'?"

What a grade-A asshole.

A slender, tired-faced officer who looked a lot like Steve Buscemi with a goatee came into the foyer. He regarded me with a steely-eyed stare. I was trying really hard not to laugh because now I was thinking of the movie *Fargo* and this Officer Aimaro guy getting force-fed into a wood chipper.

"Stalker givin' ya grief, kid?" Officer Aimaro asked.

I mean, I am definitely not a kid, but due to my constant existential crisis with getting older and closer to the great gig in the sky, I'd call being labeled one a win. Especially by a dude that looks like Steve Buscemi.

"You got that right, Officer," I replied. "This, uhh... *thing*... there's no telling what it'll—"

"Save it for my office, kid. We'll discuss the details there. C'mon, follow me."

He did an about-face and was off. I followed him and noticed Mr. Handlebar 'Stache giving me the stink eye out of my peripheral vision. Yeah whatever, get back to your busy-work papers, Officer Hardly Workin'.

Officer Aimaro's office turned out to be this shabby little glorified cubicle in a corner. The desk—

if you can even call it that, it was more like one of those plastic folding tables you'd see at a block party supporting coleslaw and potato salad—had an obsolete computer and printer parked on it. That was it. Try for anything else and you'd be swiftly approaching twenty pounds of shit in a ten-pound bag territory.

I saw there was a battered, well-worn computer chair behind the desk which must have been Officer Aimaro's throne. And on the other side was one of those cheap flimsy plastic chairs, basically of the same caliber I recall my high-school cafeteria's chairs being. I naturally assumed that one was for me.

We took our seats, and Officer Aimaro booted up his computer. I swear, the thing looked so ancient, I was expecting my ears to get assaulted by the America Online zizzing at any moment. As the machine whirred to life, he fixed me with that steely-eyed stare once again. And I remember thinking: dude, you freaking look like Steve Buscemi, not Clint Eastwood. Give it a rest with the Dirty Harry shit. You're Mistah *Pink*!

"Alright, kid. Now for starters, what's your name?"

"Bark Mouglas."

Officer Aimaro cocked an eyebrow.

"*Bark* Mouglas you said, right? Like the shit on the outside of a tree?"

Wow, that was surprisingly the first time my name had ever been referenced to what it actually is. And that was almost poetic, too. Like, I should have been offended, but I wasn't. More like mildly impressed.

"Yes, my name is Bark. Very much like the shit on the outside of a tree."

"Unique name, never heard that before. Alright Bark, so you've got yourself a stalker situation. Let's hear it, tell me all about it. I'll stop you if I have questions or need additional clarification on anything."

I exhaled and stretched in preparation for soliloquy time.

"Man, where do I start? Okay, so long story short, I've had a pretty rough go with life for several years now. Really bad drinking problem reigned supreme for a while until I got myself cleaned up in rehab. So fast forward to recently… I moved here to Galena to give myself a new beginning, start with a clean slate, whatever you wanna call it… and it was going pretty good, ya know? But now… alright, so there's this really cute waitress at Vinnie Vanucchi's, her name's Jessica. And yeah, I kinda got a thing for her… sue me, okay?

"Anyway, things were picking up with Jessica and I really felt like I had a shot with her. Hell, she was even showing me all of her cat pics. If that's not a step in the right direction, then I don't even wanna know what is, because cats are like the secret overlords of the world. So after viewing about two hundred feline photos, I finally worked up the courage to ask Jessica out on a date. And just as I was doing it… you wanna guess what happened? This freaking L.A. Mummy just materialized out of goddamn nowhere, licking the window and doing death-metal screams. Basically acting like a total buzz-kill.

"And Jessica, thinking this jackass is with *me* or something, gets freaked out and runs off. So my chances with her went up in flames and now I'm banned from Vinnie Vanucchi's, which freaking sucks because they had the best pig trotters sauce this side of the Pacific. All because of that L.A. Mummy. *Oh!* And a few nights before all this, I'd been hearing scratching and shit outside my apartment on the balcony. At first, I thought it could have been coked-out rats, but now I'm starting to wonder. And another thing I forgot to mention! Last week on my birthday, I was downtown doing the *Joker* dance on those big concrete steps and the L.A. Mummy was watching me the whole time. And this wrestler-looking guy and his girlfriend were there, and—"

"Okay… OKAY!" Officer Aimaro interrupted, waving his arms around like one of those inflatable tube men. "Jesus, take a breath, kid! Coked-out rats? The hell's the matter with you? You can stop there, I've got some questions I need answering. First off, what is this person's name? You've been calling them *'L.A. Mummy,'* is that right?"

"Yeah, that's right. I assumed that's its name because it never says anything else."

"Okay, so the *'L.A.'* is like an acronym for their first and middle name and *'Mummy'* is their last name?"

This was an interesting new development and I had to ponder it for a moment.

"Wow, ya know I never really thought of it like that…"

"Alright whatever, I'll mark it down as that. Okay, so what does this person look like?"

Now came the fun part.

"Well let's see… it's got a giant green afro, these big baggy purple pants, pale skin, and its whole torso is wrapped up in these filthy-ass bandages."

"Oh… *kay* then. About how old would you say they are, roughly?"

I had to mull this over—I never really gave its age much thought.

"Well, let's see… I dunno, probably like nineteen or… ninety? Somewhere in there."

Officer Aimaro pulled his head back a little, frowning at me.

"Look kid, don't be screwing around with me. That does me absolutely no good, you gotta be more specific than that."

"…I don't know, he looks old enough to be dead! How's that?"

Officer Aimaro sighed.

"Okay, how tall is this person? Big, little, or what?"

"Uhh… between six and seven feet tall I'd say. Definitely taller than me, though."

Officer Aimaro rose from his chair, giving me an angry glare. Just like how Mister Pink looked with the bag of jewels when he was about to hightail it outta there.

"Alright, I think you've wasted enough of my time."

"What? *No*! I've been telling you the truth, man! This L.A. Mummy is a menace! It's only a matter of time before—"

"Green afro… and wrapped up in filthy bandages? Are you hearing yourself, kid? This is the most outlandish physical description I've ever heard in all my years. I mean, hell, you might as well be describing the goddamn Jolly Green Giant with this shit. Now come on, on your feet, let's get you out of here."

I started to panic. I had to think of something to sway Buscemi here or that restraining order was gonna be as good as toilet paper.

"Come on, Steve—I mean, Officer Aimaro! This dude is freaking hard to miss, okay? In fact, let me go grab Jessica from Vinnie Vanucchi's! She saw the L.A. Mummy, too, she can help corroborate my—"

"That would be impossible to do as she filed a restraining order against you not long before you came. You should be receiving papers in the mail about it within the next few days, actually."

Now I did get out of my chair.

"*What*?! Jessica filed a restraining order against *me*?!"

"Afraid so. I didn't handle the write-up, but I did happen to see the paperwork for it. Kind of ironic you came in so soon after, too."

"…since when is it a crime to try and ask someone out on a *date*?!"

"You'd have to ask Officer Manley out front about it. He handled the write-up."

"You mean Mr. Happy Handlebar 'Stache? No thanks, I'd rather swallow a sea urchin. You know, you guys have really been no help at all, right? If this crazy bastard ends up doing something to me, it's gonna be blood on *your* hands! Good *day*, Steve!"

And with that, I marched to the exit. And I made sure to match Handlebar 'Stache's stink-eye stare with my own on the way out, except I was so mad in that moment, I probably had the intensity of '*Here's Johnny!*' Jack Torrance. He quickly broke eye contact and went back to rummaging around with his papers. Yeah, that's what I thought, Handlebar—thanks for nothing.

CHAPTER FIVE

TARGET PRACTICE

I needed to blow off some steam after that mess, so I decided to go back to my place, grab my bow, arrows, and do some target practice for a while. Behind the apartment building is this wide-open grassy area that butts up to forest, so it's the ideal spot to pretend I'm Hawkeye for an hour or two. Plus, the worst thing I could impale would be a tree or something. But in doing so, I would be murdering my namesake—the bark of the tree. Thanks for drawing my full attention to how I am the shit on the outside of a tree, Officer Aimaro... Buscemi-lookin' ass.

I already had my target stand set up but had yet to fire any arrows. I was freaking stoked. The first one I let fly, man, it made me feel like I was on top of the whole damn world. Who would have thunk shooting arrows like an elf of Rivendell would be my happy place? Ten-year-old Bark would have thought I was such a badass. And it wasn't a bad shot either! Couple degrees more to the east and it would have been bullseye, man!

Archery has developed into my kind of therapy. It used to quell the urges I would feel whenever I craved that whiskey burn, but since then, it's graduated on to pacify any negative emotions I experience. Take it from me, if you need a clear mind, just torpedo arrows everywhere—you'll instantly feel better. But please, don't kill anybody.

I shot a couple more—not quite as impressive as the first one—when the sound of a snapping twig behind me pulled me out of my therapeutic state and back to ugly reality. I spun around like lightning with an arrow set and the drawstring pulled taut. I was ready to let this sharp sucker fly and harpoon that L.A. Mummy ass-hat right through those scuzzy bandages. I was gonna make sure it didn't even know what—

It was just beach-ball Dale looking all scared with his hands up, thinking he had been about to be skewered or something. Go figure, right? I sighed and lowered my bow, easing the tension on the drawstring. False alarm. I studied Dale and saw his fear acquiesce to anger, his beady little eyes emitting sparks and his trembling mouth frothing. Man, he must have been an ugly-ass baby at one time.

"What the hell are ya doing, Blart?!" Dale yelled, slightly slurring his speech. "I give ya the privilege to play Cowboys and Indians back here and how do ya say '*thanks, Dale?*' By nearly *shooting me with a goddamn arrow, that's how*!"

I wasn't even going to correct him on my name. The dude was half-crocked already and I knew it wouldn't have made any difference.

"Sorry, Dale… I thought you were someone—or I should say some*thing*—else. See, I've been having issues lately with this L.A. Mummy stalking me, and I tried to go to the police station to file a restrai—"

"*I don't give a shit about any of that, okay*?! You point that goddamn thing at me one more time and your ass is on the street! *Capiche*?! Now where the hell's my rent, I know you've been ducking me the last week, but now I got ya cornered! Ain't no way you're scurryin' away like a little cockroach this time, buddy!"

I knew I should have been friendlier to Officer Buscemi… then he might have given me a get-out-of-jail-free card to end this greedy bastard right here, right now. *One shot, one kill*. And don't label me a bad person for thinking that, I'd be doing the whole city a massive service. They'd probably throw a celebration of death parade.

But such is not the way of the world, unfortunately. I hear they generally frown upon that sort of thing. But still, Dale was becoming a major thorn in my ass. As if the day hadn't been shitty enough, now this boozer was trying to double-dip on rent again. Yeah, that wasn't gonna happen.

"Dale, for the umpteenth time, you already got my first month's rent with the security deposit. Like, how many times do I need to remind you before it finally seeps into your thick skull? Or rather, how many less beers do you need to drink to remember better? I've been where you're at, man, and it is not a good look, trust me."

Dale's beady eyes widened to the size of marbles.

"*Hey*! You can't talk to me like that, buddy! You live under my roof—it's my house, my rules! Try showin' a little respect once in a while, Blart! And yeah... okay, I guess I do remember the whole thing with the security deposit and the first month's rent included. But you know, I'm a successful business owner! I got a lot to deal with, so cut me a break if something slips my mind occasionally!"

Dale was getting so worked up, his face was turning this kidney bean shade of red and foam was dripping down the sides of his mouth. I hoped he had gotten a clean bill of health from his cardiologist recently, because if he dropped dead of a heart attack right now, me standing here armed with a bow would look really bad. And without that get-out-of-jail-free card, Ol' Handlebar would have a field day, which would be quite terrible, because I'm too pretty for prison.

"Yeah whatever, Dale. Listen, not to be rude or anything, but I've had like the shittiest day ever and I just wanna shoot some arrows and forget about the world for a while. So if we're good, please, just let me do my thing, okay?"

"World's a shitty place, what'd ya expect, Blart? Ain't always gonna be cake and ales! Have fun with your... Cowboys and Indians there. And remember what I said about pointing that bow at me! One more time and your shit's gonna be out by the curb, watch and see!"

I had an arrow set and the drawstring pulled tight, taking careful aim at the target.

"Won't happen again, Dale. You can take my word on it."

I let the arrow fly and it pierced the target with a *thwack*! Bullseye.

Dale looked at the target, then back at me. His eyes widened further—like the size of pennies—and his mouth was a tight line.

"Okay good, Blart. Anyway, I'll be back to—"

"My name is Bark, Dale. Not Blart like the fat mall cop, it's *Bark*, okay? Get it right."

I shot another arrow and it punctured the target a couple of millimeters to the east of the last one. Another freaking bullseye.

"Yeah… Bark. Okay, I got it."

Dale shifted his roly-poly bod uneasily before wheeling and waddling away without another word.

Good riddance, man. If I didn't know any better, I would almost think things were taking a turn for the better.

C H A P T E R   S I X

W H O ' S   T H A T   K N O C K I N G   A T M Y   D A M N   D O O R ?

After a while, I decided to call it quits on the archery and pack it all in. I went into my apartment, fixed myself some Easy Mac garnished with a couple pig trotters for dinner and washed it down with apple cider vinegar. And don't judge me for drinking it straight because the health benefits are out of this world.

As soon as dinner was devoured, I went into the living room and played some *GoldenEye* on N64 for an hour or so. That game is my freaking jam, and I'm an absolute fiend in multiplayer mode. And between shooting real-life arrows and virtual bullets, I was definitely feeling a lot better.

That is, until I heard scratching outside on the balcony.

And I realized I had left my bow outside, too. Well, shit… shoot me in the foot and call me Hullabaloo, why don't ya? I proceeded to the door with caution, but

I didn't want to jump to any conclusions. Officer Aimaro may not have believed me about the coked-out rats, but I've seen 'em with my own eyes. Literally *bet money* on which one would tear out the other's insides faster, too. Dark times, man… dark times. They do exist, and they are not to be taken lightly.

However, there also loomed the possibility of that hare-brained L.A. Mummy being out there, scratching up a tizzy. Yeah, that would be terrible. I think I'd take a horde of coked-out rats over the L.A. Mummy any day of the week. Jesus, of all the nights to leave my bow outside, it had to freaking be this one. So much for things taking a turn for the better, right?

Then I thought, *what the hell am I doing*? If the L.A. Mummy *is* out there treating my place like a scratching post, I'd better arm myself with *something*. I pictured those four vampire-like teeth protruding from its mouth like tusks and shuddered. Yeah, a weapon was most definitely a must.

I did an about-face and set off to find something. The scratching, clawing, whatever it was, kept on going. It had no sense of rhythm either, like that shit-faced guy you'd see at a bar tapping his hand to the music, except he's always a couple beats behind. I perused the kitchen, inspecting my knives, but they were all dull AF. Whatever, better than nothing, right? I selected the biggest one, which looked like the lame butter-knife cousin to Michael Myers's butcher knife, and slowly made my way to the door.

I swear, as soon as I put my hand on the knob, the scratching stopped, like whatever was out there knew. Like it was anticipating and preparing for this big showdown and knew I was about to enter the ring, and the only thing standing between us was this cheap flimsy door.

A sudden series of thumping noises made my heart pole vault to my throat.

I flung open the door, roaring the most ferocious primal scream I could muster while ready to bludgeon whatever was there with my glorified butter knife. There was nothing on the balcony, but when I stepped out and glanced down, I caught a quick flash of green disappearing around the corner of the building to the back. I felt a technicolor yawn threatening to surface, but I forcefully swallowed it down.

The L.A. Mummy.

The green must have been its dumbass 'fro wobbling as it fled. So it knew where I lived then. This was exactly what I did *not* want to happen, and in a moment of fiery passion, I bounded down the stairs after this lunatic.

This was going to freaking end *now*.

I came around the building to the wide-open grassy plain; I could just make out streaks of green and purple slipping into the woods, which was actually wise of the L.A. Mummy, because I was feeling mad as a hatter and my bow was lying only a few feet away now.

I sprinted over, dropping the butter knife for the bow, and immediately set an arrow and pulled back the drawstring. I scanned the treeline while taking aim, ready to unleash a hailstorm of arrows.

"Alright, L.A. Mummy! I know you can hear me

in there, so listen up! If I catch you prowling around again, I am going to go full Legolas on your filthy ass, and you're gonna come out looking like the world's most hideous pin cushion, okay?! And I will not hesitate! Because you've successfully made my life here absolute hell! You've been stalking me, you ruined my chances of going out with Jessica from Vinnie Vannuchi's—*and* subsequently got me banned from there I might add!—and now you're at my goddamn apartment in the dead of night clawing the siding and shit! I mean, what the hell do you want from me, man?! *Just let me live my fucking life in peace*!"

There was silence, save for a few crickets chirping. And then…

"L.A. MUMMY!"

The death-metal shriek cut through the air like a knife slicing open a fish belly. Even the crickets got spooked and shut up. I never, even in my wildest nightmares, thought '*L.A. Woman'* could ever sound so unsettling, but after that moment, I was a believer. I will never listen to that Doors song again, and if I happen to see Jim Morrison in the afterlife, I'm gonna give him a swift kick in the nuts.

Staunch yet unnerved, I held my position, prepared to fire at any sign of movement. But there was nothing—no shuffling, no crunching leaves, no ghoulish warbling… nothing. And after a couple of minutes, the crickets resumed their happy trilling and everything seemed to revert to how it was, as if the L.A. Mummy had never been here in the first place.

I knew better, though. I was smarter than those

dopey crickets frolicking about in bug's life La-La Land. I knew there was a mummy maniac out there in those woods, standing still as death and blending in amongst the murk of the wilderness, watching me. And I remember thinking, *you like what you see, asshole? Go ahead, keep on staring, because I'm not gonna let you scamper out of this situation, not on my watch.* The L.A. Mummy had taken this shit too far, and I was ready to stand sentry all night if that's what it took. It had to move at some point, and when that time came, I'd be on it like flies on shit. Or at least my arrows would be.

To pass the time and keep myself sharp and alert, I started shooting at the target stand. And damn, I was accruing bullseyes up the wazoo—I was imagining the bullseye as that stupid green afro, so that kept the motivational juices flowing. After a while, the target got so filled it started to look like Pinhead; I quickly went and retrieved all the arrows before legions of chains could fly out and tear my soul apart. I remained vigilant the entire time, too, and I did not see nor hear anything wicked this way coming. How the hell could someone stay in the same spot for so long, completely unmoving? Bad vibes, man.

CHAPTER SEVEN

BEST FREAKING WEDDING EVER

Eventually, I had no choice but to abandon my post and get ready for work. And let me tell you, after being awake all night, I definitely felt like something of a mummy myself. The worst part was, I had a big wedding to run sound for at the hotel, so calling last minute and taking a sick day was unfortunately not an option. Adulting sucks the big one. Thanks for once again making my life exponentially more difficult, you L.A. Mummy jackass.

As I retreated to the apartment building, the only sound I heard was a choir of birds singing an entrance theme for the rising sun. No L.A. Mummy, thankfully. It looked like the freaky bastard would live to do karaoke from hell another day. Oh, and stalk the shit out of people, too. Saved by the work grind…

Truth be told, work turned out to be surprisingly spectacular. While ensuring optimal audio on no sleep is not something I would recommend trying at home, everything proceeded according to plan. It may not seem important, but think about it—the music, loved ones' speeches, and even the dorky emcee—those are crucial components to a wedding. And the coolest part? I got to bear witness to the best damn wedding *ever*. It was a freaking *Halloween-themed* wedding, which has always been my dream! Every guest was dressed in costume. I saw Ghostface, Bob Ross, Princess Leia, Buddy the Elf, and even Spike Spiegel to name a few.

But what really rocked my socks were the bride and groom. The bride wore this gorgeous, flowing black dress, and the groom was dressed as John Hurt's doomed character from *Alien*! I kid you not, this dude had the alien jutting out of his chest and everything! And he recited his vows at the altar looking like that, too! I know it may sound cliché, but this wedding was truly *magical*, and it made me feel several shades of warm and fuzzy inside that I could play a part in making it all possible. I felt like what I did really had a purpose, helping make people's dreams come alive on their special day.

And that's what it should be all about, you know? Making as many people happy as you can in your own way. Because there's enough darkness and depression in the world already to feed endless boogeymen a bajillion times over. Believe me, in my worst inebriated throes, I experienced some of the absolute blackest of that darkness in places I wouldn't even bring someone's hamster nowadays. And much to my regret, I know I've contributed to some of that darkness as well. And who knows? Maybe the L.A. Mummy is one of those pain-eating boogeymen, and like the Pied Piper, has come to collect a long-overdue debt from me.

Whatever the case, that's all in the past and I'm a different person now. For the better, too, a thousandfold. Seeing the elated faces of the bride and groom on their best day made me realize I do make a difference. I have changed. I am indeed that reborn phoenix rising from the steaming pile of shit. And you know what? No matter what occurred in the past, I don't deserve to be chased all over God's green Earth by some L.A. Mummy sonofabitch. I also don't deserve to be perpetually heckled by dumbass drunken Dale, who can't remember the last time he was sober, let alone that I already paid him rent. And I certainly don't deserve to be given the stink eye and disbelieving riot act by a handlebar-mustache deputy dawg and Buscemi-ass looking cop.

I wasn't going to let all of that keep me down, especially on a day as amazing as a Halloween wedding. And damn, if I would have known beforehand, you better believe I would have come to work dressed up as freaking Beetlejuice or the Joker— the bigwigs never divulge the good stuff... damn killjoys. Regardless, I had to commend the stars of the show for the world's coolest wedding, and I quickly spotted 'em moseying off the dancefloor for a breather. They smiled at me as I approached.

"Hi, I'm Bark! I organized all of the sound and audio. I just wanted to say... that this is the best *fucking* wedding I have ever seen. And with my job, I see a lot of weddings. Seriously, good on you guys, and congratulations."

"Oh my god! Thank you so much! And thank you for all the work you did, everything's been so perfect!" the bride exclaimed.

"Yeah thanks, man!" the groom said. "It's really been the best day!"

They kissed, the protruding alien acting as an awkward third wheel.

"You guys look awesome, would you mind if I got a quick picture with ya?" I asked.

They happily obliged and I selfie'd it, the three of us putting on our goofiest faces possible. I still have that photo, and whenever I feel doubtful of myself or my profession, I look back at that picture. It never ceases to bolster my spirits and remind me why I love what I do.

The rest of the wedding went off without a hitch, the crowd of crazy cosplayers having the time of their lives. Seriously, best event ever, that was one for the books. And since it started in the morning and finished up around midday, I was out of work by early afternoon.

I checked my phone and saw Larry had tried calling a couple of times. I called back, and he picked up about halfway through the first ring.

"Yo, Bark! Where the hell you at, man? I've been trying to get a hold of ya! I think I'm at the right place? Can you come outside really quick to make sure, though?"

I shook my head because this was typical Larry at

his finest. So much for him giving me a heads up.

"Dude, Larry, I've been at work this whole morning! What the hell happened to you telling me when you were leaving?"

"Well, you know how it is, man. I got a bug up my ass, left late yesterday, and drove through the night. Speaking of which, are you coming home soon or what? I need at least three pots of coffee *stat* before I turn into a zombie."

"No mention of zombies, mummies, or anything of the ilk, okay? That's a touchy subject for me currently. And also, lucky for you, I'm just wrapping up here, so I'll be back in a few."

"Oh shit, that's right! I forgot about your stalker dilemma! Were you able to get the restraining order or what?"

"I'll tell you about it when I get there, I'm heading out now. See ya soon, dude."

I ended the call, feeling a titch peeved. That was so like Larry, compulsive as a mad dog chasing a squirrel. What kind of psycho journeys hundreds of miles through the night, thereby planning to exist into the next day dependent on copious amounts of caffeine? Larry, that's who—I am surrounded by maniacs. I guess driving through the day like a normal person and having a warm bed waiting for you is overrated or something. Fortunately, I got out of work earlier than usual, otherwise his Eager McBeaver ass would have sat there for hours. And whatever, let him stew for a while. However, a few pots of coffee sounded glorious; Larry wasn't the only one running on no sleep after all.

I trudged back to my place and saw Larry's black Chevy Equinox parked in the lot. It's easy to spot because he's got a *Wayne Enterprises* sticker just under the back window. It didn't look like he was in his car, though, so I glanced about, thinking he maybe had to take a leak or stretch his legs.

"Hey, B-Mougz!"

Only Larry would devise an appellation as absurd as that, so I spun and caught him peeking from the side of my building like he was trying to hide. He looked like that goofy Kilroy cartoon with only his eyes and nose visible.

"Larry, what the hell are you doing?" I asked as I made my way to him.

"Um, well… I think I met your asshole landlord."

"You met Dale?"

"Well, he came up to my car and drunkenly pounded on the window demanding rent money… so if you wanna call that meeting someone, then I guess?"

"...and you're hiding because of Dale's drunk ass?" I asked. "The guy's built like a scoop of melted ice cream, dude, clean his damn clock. He's the least of any concerns around here."

"Speaking of concerns, tell me what happened with that restraining order while I bring my stuff in."

I helped Larry bring his luggage up to my apartment while I explained my marvelous misadventures with Handlebar and Buscemi, and the ill-fated restraining order that never saw the light of day.

"Alright, that settles it then," Larry said as I finished. "You're bringing your bow along wherever we go."

"No way, I've got a reputation around here, dude! I can't just go waltzing around town with my bow and arrow like I'm freaking Robin Hood or something."

Larry shook his head.

"Okay, Mr. Golden Reputation. If you're not going to protect your guest of honor, at least brew me a pot of coffee. Please and thank you."

I happily obliged.

CHAPTER EIGHT

IT AIN'T NO STARLIT TOOTLE DOWN RAINBOW ROAD

After our caffeine fix, we set out downtown for some grub. As we walked, I kept tabs on our surroundings. Maybe I should have brought that damn bow along for peace of mind.

"So did you watch it yet?" Larry asked.

"...huh?"

"That movie I was telling you about! With the giant teleporting man-child hammering everybody into hamburger meat!"

I spotted a glimpse of green, but it was just some beardo with a lime-colored parakeet on his shoulder.

"Uhh... yeah, I watched it," I said. "It was okay... I mean, I wouldn't take a bullet for it or anything, but it was decent."

Larry gaped at me.

"Wait, what? Take a *bullet*? …it's just a movie, man!"

"Well, no shit."

"So what the hell movie *would* you take a bullet for?"

I pondered this for a moment, but the answer came pretty quick.

"I dunno, *The Shining*'s a really good movie, dude."

"You're batshit insane," Larry said.

I shrugged and we ambled along. Just up ahead on the left was—

"Hey, Vinnie Vannuchi's!" Larry exclaimed. "That's the Italian place you told me about! Man, I could really go for some lasagna. How 'bout we—"

"No, I'm banned from there, dude! That was where Jessica and the L.A. Mummy… okay, never mind, long story. Nevertheless, we can't go there."

"So much for your reputation around here, huh?"

I heard Larry's smartass remark, but I didn't even care; I was more focused on what was ahead—those legendary concrete stairs. And what stood on them was what made the hairs on my neck stand up.

The L.A. Mummy.

It was expressionless and unmoving, staring right at me.

"So where can we go inste—*Ah!* What the hell, Bark!"

Not realizing I'd stopped, Larry had bumped into me.

"Larry, turn around right now, we're going back to my place."

"But I'm hungry like the wolf! Why can't—"

"I've got Easy Mac and pig trotters, you'll be fine. Let's go!"

"But…"

Larry shut up when he followed my gaze and saw the L.A. Mummy standing stiff as a poker, glaring at us. It didn't take him long to hypothesize who this freakshow was.

"I *told* you ya shoulda brought the fucking bow!" Larry said.

Before I could respond, the L.A. Mummy sprung to life like someone flipped its switch. And this maniac, well, it busted out into the goddamn *Joker* dance. We watched in horror as this thing reenacted the moves *flawlessly,* still maintaining eye contact with us. The green afro gyrated and the samurai pants roiled like purple waves. I could see its quad of razor-sharp canines gleaming in the sunlight at certain moments, too. Did this thing seriously master the whole *Joker* dance after watching me do it *one time*?

Honestly, I didn't want to stick around to find out.

I wrangled Larry and we got the hell out of there, making a mad dash for my place. I didn't check to see if it was following us or not. We played a desperate game of *Frogger* through traffic and people, never stopping once. When we got to my building, we were panting like a couple of overheated dogs. We leaned against the wooden stairs to catch our breath. I looked where we came from, but I didn't see or hear anything—it didn't appear like we had been followed.

"That was all kinds of screwed up, dude…" Larry said, gasping for breath. "What the hell was that freak even doing?"

I took a few gulps of air, trying to steady my breathing.

"The *Joker* dance," I replied. "You know, from the movie with Joaquin Phoenix. It was watching me when I did it on my birthday, and I think it's trying to mock me now. Or maybe it's a big fan, too, I dunno…"

"Wait, you were doing the *Joker* dance in public? In front of the whole damn *town*?!"

"Yeah, it was sort of like a birthday present to myself. At least until the wrestler dude and his girlfriend stopped me."

"Wow… *alrighty then*," Larry replied, reminding me of Ace Ventura. "Well, I stand by what I told you before—this is like a shitty horror movie or something."

I nodded, scanning the distance for any glimpse of green or purple.

"Can we *please* go inside?" Larry asked. "Because if I see that thing galumphing at us while doing that manic mambo, I'm gonna shit my pants."

We made our way up the stairs and into my apartment. I locked the door, but immediately thought I should have installed one of those chain things on the door like I'd wanted. And not just for Dale, we had more pressing issues now. My Mouglas sense was tingling, and it felt like we were experiencing the calm before the storm.

But before we did anything else, I brewed another pot of coffee.

We sat on rickety stools at my kitchen island— actually, I would say it was more like a peninsula— sipping our java delights.

"So how's the sober life been treating ya?" Larry asked.

Funny that he'd pop a question like that as I'm savoring the coffee's burn.

"It ain't no starlit tootle down Rainbow Road, I can tell you that much. But, things are definitely a lot better now than they were before, dude. I'm just trying to take it a day at a time, ya know?"

Larry smiled and nodded.

"I'm happy for you, man, I really am," he replied. "And look, I'm sorry I wasn't there for you more before. I should have seen the signs. I dunno, I should have—"

"Dude, thank you, but shut up. I was great at hiding it, there was nothing you or anyone could have done differently—don't even think twice about it. I sought the help I needed, and that is freaking that. We're all good, Larry. I'm just glad you're here."

He looked down into the black void of his coffee.

"I'm happy to hear that, Bark. And I'm really glad

to be here, even considering the… well, circumstances. I mean, *hell*! You take the bull by the horns with your drinking and get sober, which is nothing short of admirable by the way, yet now there's this *Joker*-dancing mummy freak following you around like a dark storm cloud. That's just… well, for lack of a better word… it's *shitty*!"

"Yeah no kidding, Larry. Try living it."

"I think I'm good, man. But aside from that, you seem to be doing pretty well for yourself out here! I'm proud of ya, Bark, I really am!"

"Thanks, dude. That means a lot."

We took a few sips of our coffee in silence. Then Larry slapped his hand on the table.

"Alrighty, enough of this mawkish crap. How about some dinner, eh?"

"Oh man, I have a treat for you, hang on…"

I got up and retrieved a jar of pig trotters from the fridge. I slid it across the countertop to Larry along with a plate and a spoon.

"Go crazy. I've got some Easy Mac and maybe a Hot Pocket or two if you want that as well."

Larry unscrewed the cap and looked inside the jar, immediately grimacing like he got slapped in the face with a wet fart.

"Damn, Bark! What the hell is this smelly garbage?! They look like little feet!"

"Yeah, they're pig trotters, dude. They're pickled—"

"*Pig's feet*?!"

Larry's face turned pale and he swiftly screwed the cap on, sliding the jar back to me.

"I think I'm good with just a Hot Pocket, man, thanks."

I unearthed two Hot Pockets from the freezer and zapped 'em in the microwave.

"What do ya want to drink? I've got some apple cider vinegar or water."

Larry looked like he had sucked a lemon dry.

"...apple cider *vinegar*?! Shit, just gimme water, man."

I assembled our makeshift smorgasbord and dinner was served—a Hot Pocket topped with a couple pig trotters and a glass of apple cider vinegar for me, and a Hot Pocket, plain, with a glass of water for Larry.

"This is a momentous event, dude," I said. "First meal I'm sharing with someone in my new place. Feels bloody awesome, too."

Larry raised his glass of water, and I followed suit with my glass of apple cider vinegar.

"Cheers, man!"

"Cheers, dude!"

Right as our glasses clinked, the front door banged violently in its frame. We set our drinks down and stared in bewilderment.

With a splintered yawn, the door swung open.

CHAPTER NINE

L.A. MUMMY!

In the threshold was Dale, drunk as a trolleyed skunk, his watermelon physique swaying to and fro.

"...and *now* I've got da' both of yuz!" Dale slurred, "...right where I want ya!"

We jumped from our stools.

"Is this sloshed sonofabitch for real?" Larry asked. "He just smashed open your door, man! He can't *do* that!"

"Dale!" I yelled. "What the hell are you doing?! You can't just boogie your way in here whenever you feel like it! We're in the middle of goddamn dinner!"

Dale staggered into the room, wobbling precariously. I had no idea how he hadn't fallen on his ass yet. Somehow, he managed to slam the door behind him for dramatic effect.

He pointed at Larry.

"*You*—you thought you was all cute… with your bitches over on… on Hollywood *Booguh-lard*! Thought you could slip through the… the *cracks*, huh? *Well I don't think so, buddy!* You gonna pay your *rent*, cockroach!"

"I don't even live here, you jackass!" Larry said.

Apparently satisfied, Dale switched his drunken wrath to me, his glossy eyes rolling around in their sockets like caster wheels.

"And *you*! Where's your arrows now, Blart? Cuz I—cuz I don't *see* 'em anywhere! Little boy Cupid ain't so… so tough without his *bow*, huh?"

He started laughing, which caused him to finally fall on his ass. He looked like an obese turtle on its back, wheezing as his short limbs flailed about.

I was pissed, like blood-boiling level pissed, and I marched to Dale's overturned form, crouched down, and got right in his ugly mug.

"Dale, get up and waddle your drunk ass outta here right *now*! This is pathetic, I mean, *look* at yourself for Christ's sake! You look like Patrick Star on ecstasy!"

Something must have clicked in Dale's inebriated brain because he scrambled to his feet—took him *several* attempts, too—and came so close our faces were inches apart. And holy *hell*, his breath smelled like a rancid Porta-John.

"I—I want my *money*, dammit! I *need* it! I… I lost my ass on those… damn horses again, Blart! *You gotta pay me!*"

"Look, dude, it's not even the next month yet, so—

"

I was interrupted by the front window shattering, showering us with bits of glass. I saw a green form cannonballing into the room just as I covered my face.

"No, no, no… *shit*!" Larry exclaimed.

I uncovered my face and saw a green afro, grimy bandages, and purple samurai pants.

The L.A. Mummy stood in the room, its four vampire-like teeth revealed through its ghastly grin.

"*L.A. MUMMY*!" it shrieked.

And just like that, we were caught in the midst of the storm again.

"*HEY!*" Dale thundered. "That ain't no door, you stupid motherfucker! That's a goddamn *window*! …*MY goddamn window*! You're gonna *pay* for that, you circus freak bastard!"

Dale was so fired up, his face had turned an alarming shade of violet, making him look like Grimace. I could see the veins popping out of his neck like tree roots.

The L.A. Mummy observed Dale, its head cocked slightly as it studied his throbbing neck veins.

"Well? Don't just stand there like a goddamn putz!" Dale said. "I'll take cash or check! Gimme a—"

"*L.A. MUMMY*!"

The L.A. Mummy vaulted through the air and latched onto Dale's rotund form, looking like a massive, pied parasite.

It bared its four large canines and chomped into Dale's neck.

"*Oh sweet Jesus!*" Dale wailed.

The razor-sharp teeth slashed through the meat of his neck as the L.A. Mummy bit down completely and tore away a large chunk of flesh.

"*HOLY GOD!*" Larry exclaimed, putting his hands on his cheeks like the *Home Alone* movie cover.

A stream of blood blasted from Dale's heinous wound, painting the wall a wet crimson. The L.A. Mummy detached itself from Dale and stared at the flowing gore like a hungry mutt would ogle a slab of raw meat.

"*AHHHHH!! OH JEEEEESUS!*" Dale screeched.

He vainly tried plugging the wound with his hand to squelch the squirting, but it was no use—the poor bastard was missing a good quarter of his neck. Dale ran back and forth, screaming his head off.

The L.A. Mummy followed his every move, keeping itself directly in the trajectory of Dale's arterial spray. The maniac hopped up and down with glee as the blood saturated its body, even sticking its tongue out to lap some up like a child would with falling snowflakes.

"*Holy shit, Bark!*" Larry cried, "We gotta *do* something! Call the freaking cops!"

I nodded and pulled my phone out. As morbid as the scene was, I couldn't help but feel amused at the thought of Handlebar and Buscemi walking into this bloodbath and seeing the looks on their faces.

"*HELP ME*! *Somebody HELP ME*!" Dale screamed, running about and slathering the room with his blood. The L.A. Mummy was bouncing in tune with Dale and trying to gulp as much of the gore as possible.

"Nine-one-one, what is your emergency?" a cool female voice asked from my phone.

"Yeah, hi," I replied. "My name is Bark Mouglas, is Handlebar or Buscemi around? This is *important*!"

"...I... I don't... sir, what is your emergency? Do I hear yelling?"

"*Look*, I tried to tell your numbskull deputy dawgs that this L.A. Mummy was gonna do some heavy, dirty shit, okay? *And nobody would listen!* Now it's broken into my apartment and it's murdering my landlord Dale and *drinking his goddamn blood, too! What the fuck kind of mummy even drinks blood anyway?!*"

"Sir! I need you to calm dow—"

"Calm? *How's this for fucking calm, huh?!* Listen to this *shit!*"

I held the phone out to relay the hellish scene unfurling.

"*AaAAgghhHh!*"

Dale, having lost so much blood, moved sluggishly now and was wailing these piercing animalistic shrieks no human should ever make. The L.A. Mummy, drenched from afro to toe in Dale's blood, was bobbing about and whooping like a howler monkey.

"...oh, my *Lord…*" the female voice on the phone said, her voice quavering.

Larry dashed over and bellowed into the phone's receiver.

"Send us some goddamn help NOW!"

As Larry got close, a foul odor wafted up, invading my nostrils, and I scrunched my face in disgust.

He looked at me sheepishly.

"Sorry, man… I shit my pants, *I couldn't help it!*"

Hey, given the circumstances, I couldn't fault him.

"Hello… *HELLO!*" the voice in the phone said. "Units are en route! Please get yourself to a safe location and stay on the line with—"

"Thank you, gotta go!" I yelled, ending the call and dropping my phone.

Dale had lost consciousness and was lying on the floor, most likely dead; his arterial spray had lessened to a weak, sporadic spurting of blood, which the L.A. Mummy was gleefully slurping like a water fountain.

I looked at Larry, who was watching the grisly display with glass-eyed horror. He seemed to be about a hair's width away from entering a catatonic state.

"...*Larry!*" I whisper-shouted.

His eyes returned to normal and he glanced over, his mouth slightly agape.

"I think as long as that blood keeps squirting, this nutcase is gonna stay occupied," I whispered, *"So now's our chance, let's go! C'mon!"*

Larry nodded and I yanked his arm, leading us to the door. I half-ass looked at the L.A. Mummy as we passed, but it was completely absorbed in its task, making sure to consume every last drop of blood—if it did notice us fleeing, it didn't show any signs. We pushed through the door and scrambled down the stairs to the parking lot. I was hoping to see flashing blue and red lights approaching in the distance, but no such luck.

Larry was coated with Dale's blood, and after examining myself, I was definitely no better. But we weren't totally free from the woods yet.

We needed to nope the fuck outta there.

Let Handlebar and Buscemi deal with the L.A. Mummy, that was their job after all, right? Larry and I had seen a shit-load more than we ever bargained for, we should be allowed to—

CRACK!

The sound of the flimsy front door ripping from its frame pierced the night like a firecracker at a funeral. The door arced through the air and landed right at our feet with a thud. A little further, and it would have decapitated us like a blade through butter.

"L.A. MUMMY!"

The shriek came from the balcony, and I could see a dark form in the doorway, silhouetted against the light from inside my apartment.

Well, more like an abattoir now really.

"Larry, c'mon! Unlock your car, let's book it outta here!"

Larry patted his pockets, and his face took on a grim, ashen pallor.

"Shit, man... *I left 'em back in your place!* What the hell are we gonna do?!"

Typical Larry... one job to do and he royally fucked it up. I looked up at the L.A. Mummy, still standing in the doorway.

I could feel it glaring at me.

"We fight, dude," I responded to Larry, not taking my gaze off of the shadowy figure above. "We're gonna run to the backyard. I left my bow out there. Let's see how animated this bloody lunatic is after it gets skewered with a few arrows, eh?"

Larry gave a quick nod.

"Let's *GO!*" I roared.

We sprinted across the pavement toward the back of the building.

"*L.A. MUMMY!*"

I heard the death-metal shriek behind us followed by a thumping sound of what I assumed to be the L.A. Mummy landing on the asphalt.

We raced across the grass and I could see the target stand with my bow and quiver of arrows leaning against its side.

Almost there.

"Oh shit, man, *it's coming for us!*" Larry cried, "I shoulda worn a damn *turtleneck*!"

I didn't look back to see how close it was, but I heard the stampeding of its footfalls. I could have sworn I heard multiple ploddings, like it was freaking barreling on all fours or something.

Arriving at the target stand, I snatched up my bow and set an arrow in record time. I saw the L.A. Mummy up a ways, not quite as close as I would have figured it to be. But out in the open and with the moon illuminating the grassy plain, the L.A. Mummy was on full display.

"Oh, *fuck...*" Larry moaned.

The L.A. Mummy must have ditched the afro and samurai pants in my apartment. The loss of the 'fro revealed the disturbing face; it had no hair whatsoever—none atop its head and no eyebrows. Its dead, shark-like eyes were maroon in color and the size of checkers pieces. Without the pants, its entire body from shoulder to calf was shown to be wrapped in the dirty bandages, completely soaked with Dale's blood.

The four bared canine teeth glistened red in the moonlight.

And then it held something up in the air, sort of proudly, like it was the Holy Grail. I squinted my eyes to see what it was, but my vision sucks.

"...is that your *phone*, man?!" Larry asked.

At least Larry was good for something. And yeah, he was right, I could tell from the boxy contours it had to be my phone—also because my pockets were empty. I must have dropped it at some point inside.

The L.A. Mummy, still staring at us with that shit-eating—or rather *blood*-eating—grin, made a few taps on my phone's screen. Then, thundering percussion boomed from the speaker followed by a staccato chant of *'hey!'s* as it tossed my phone to the grassy space between us, allowing the music to score the scene.

Goddammit, it was *'The Hey Song.'*

I knew what was coming next.

"Shoot it, man! *What the hell are you waiting for?!*" Larry exclaimed.

'The Hey Song' intensified and the L.A. Mummy broke out into the *Joker* dance just as I fired the first arrow—it twirled out of the way at the last moment.

"Again! *Keep shooting!*" Larry cried.

I shot several more arrows amidst the rowdy *'hey!'s* and shuffling melody—every time, the L.A. Mummy pirouetted out of the way like the world's most hideous ballerina. I was getting unnerved and needed to concentrate. I knew this goddamn dance as well as freaking Joaquin Phoenix did and I had to focus.

I studied the pattern of its movements for a few seconds, getting a feel for the dance and involuntarily moving along to the music, while still keeping aim.

And I was locked into the groove now, baby.

I followed the L.A. Mummy's gallivant and spin, feigning like I was going to fire.

…but I moved a couple degrees to the west at the

last moment, anticipating that awkward thrust as the next progression and let the drawstring snap, the arrow whizzing into the night and…

Bullseye.

The fletching of the arrow protruded from the center of the L.A. Mummy's chest—it reminded me of the alien bursting from John Hurt's ribcage in *Alien*, like that badass groom's wedding attire. It looked like the point went in pretty deep, too, with a good quarter of the shaft buried into the bandages and beyond.

'The Hey Song' blared its final chorus of '*hey!'s* and ended.

"Yes… *YES!*" Larry said, "Eat that, you mummy sonofabitch!"

As I focused on the arrow, I quickly came to a gut-wrenching realization—there was no fresh blood blossoming around the L.A. Mummy's wound. The bandages were saturated with gore, but it was all Dale's.

The L.A. Mummy dipped its head to examine the arrow lodged in its chest, then slowly lifted its face, glaring at us with a crooked smirk. It gripped the arrow and ripped it from its body, creating a squelching sound like a smashed rotten tomato. The wound looked like a little nail hole you'd see in a wall where a picture used to hang. But still, no fresh blood was spilling out.

How the *hell* was this possible?

The L.A. Mummy dropped the arrow to the grass and took a step toward us. I heard Larry whimper next to me.

Suddenly, we were blinded by a light.

Chapter Ten

Man, I Fucking Hate That Guy

"*Hey!* Who's down there?" a voice asked—it sounded like it came from the side of the building. "And who the hell was blasting that stupid NBA music? *God*, I hate that song…"

As my eyes acclimated, I could see a large form pointing a flashlight at us from the parking lot.

"I'm Officer Manley!" the form shouted. "Got a call there was some kinda disturbance over here. One of you make the call? Cuz this better be good, my shift was s'pposed to be done already."

Handlebar.

Where the hell was Buscemi at? Because if there was ever a time for some wannabe Dirty Harry shit, it was *now*.

Handlebar sashayed toward us, keeping the flashlight in our direction.

"What're you dipshits doing out here so late anyway? And why did—"

Handlebar stopped when he was about ten yards away from the L.A. Mummy—who was closest—and surveyed it with the light.

His eyes popped and the handlebar mustache wiggled.

"What sorta fucked-up dimeshow attraction you s'pposed to be?! And *shit*… is that…"

He half-ass scanned Larry and I with the flashlight, too.

"Christ Almighty… *you're all covered in blood!*"

Handlebar retreated a few steps.

"I… I heard of this before… you're all in one of them… *Satanic cults!* Sacrifices and shit! My *God*… I… I…"

I advanced a few steps.

"Handlebar, you've got it all wrong! It's the goddamn L.A. Mummy here, it killed Dale—he's in my apartment, dead as a doornail! And now it—"

"Y'all sacrificed *Dale?!*" Handlebar exclaimed, drawing his gun.

Larry and I immediately put our hands up. The L.A. Mummy stood there with that crooked grin.

I felt the beam of the flashlight assault my face and had to close my eyes.

"*You!*" Handlebar said. "I remember you—you were just in the station! I knew you was no good then, but *Christ!* I *never* woulda guessed… all *this*!"

"Bark was at the station trying to prevent this from happening, you bastard!" Larry yelled. "But none of you would *listen* to him!"

"*Hey!* Shut up, *Satanist!*" Handlebar said. "You can't talk to me like that! Don't move, none of ya!"

Dropping the flashlight, his now-empty hand seized the walkie-talkie at his belt and brought it to his face.

"I—I need some backup out here at Dale's *NOW!* There's these three… *devil-worshippers!* All covered in blood, and they mighta—"

"*L.A. MUMMY!*"

The L.A. Mummy leapt at Handlebar like a jackrabbit, making contact with his midsection. Handlebar gave a surprised *oomf!* as the gun and radio flew out of his hands and he was knocked to the grass, the L.A. Mummy landing on top of him.

The L.A. Mummy's evil grin widened to the edges of its face, revealing the wicked, bloodied vampire teeth.

"*Holy FUCK!*" Handlebar wailed. "The *devil! You're the goddamn devil!* You're—"

Handlebar was interrupted as the L.A. Mummy sank its fangs into his expansive belly. It shook its head back and forth like a mad dog—the ensuing sounds of ripping flesh were like those of tearing moist cardboard.

Handlebar's eyes bugged out and he belched a

fountain of blood.

The L.A. Mummy burrowed its face into the sizable crater it had made in Handlebar, enjoying a buffet of his guts. Handlebar's siren-like, high-pitched screams blared amidst wet smacking noises from the L.A. Mummy's feasting.

"Bark…" Larry said. "We—we gotta help him… we gotta do *something*…"

I heard a thud as Larry dropped to his knees, overcome by the grisly scene. And I felt in the same boat, too—completely frozen, rooted to the spot. I had never heard a person make those sort of screams before; they were the desperate screeches I would expect a rodent to cry as a cat playfully tore it to pieces.

Thankfully, the screams didn't last long, and they eventually ceased. The wet smacking continued, but then, that stopped, too.

Which meant the L.A. Mummy was done.

And it would come for us again.

Sure enough, the L.A. Mummy lifted its head from the gory cavity and stretched to its feet. It turned—its entire body coated with blood and pulpy bits—and smiled, the dripping fangs bared. It cocked its head to one side.

"*L.A. MUMMY!*" it shrieked, in the death-metal timbre nightmares are made of.

And then it sauntered forward.

Larry fell on his ass and started crab-walking backwards.

"Oh, *God*... please, *no!*" Larry whimpered.

The L.A. Mummy trudged ahead, its head still cocked.

So it all came down to this then.

So be it.

Fuck, I needed a drink.

I held my position and raised the bow, nocking an arrow and taking aim.

Thwack!

The first arrow flew and pierced the L.A. Mummy in its right shoulder. Unaffected, it kept advancing, its glassy maroon eyes fixed on me.

I snatched another arrow, nocked it, and pulled the drawstring taut.

"*Bark!*" Larry wailed, still crab-walking backwards. "What the hell are you *doing, man?! Get the fuck away from it!*"

Thwack!

The second arrow impacted where the maniac's heart should be. Again, nothing—it shuffled ahead.

Moving like a well-oiled machine, I set another arrow—the sonofabitch was only a couple of yards away.

Thwack!

Bullseye, right between the eyes.

The L.A. Mummy stopped and comically crossed its eyes upwards to stare at the arrow jutting out of its forehead.

I lowered my bow.

If that wouldn't hit its off switch, I don't know what would.

But then.

The L.A. Mummy did a wheezy laugh, clasped the arrow, and plucked it out of its forehead with a wet sucking sound.

I heard scurrying behind me, probably Larry abandoning me... asshole. Whatever, at least one of us could get out of this with their organs still intact.

Grinning, the L.A. Mummy traipsed onward, now raising the removed arrow above its head—this honorless shit stain was really gonna try to kill me with my own weapon. I assumed a stance, ready to battle to the last breath, ready to—

"*Bark... DUCK!*" Larry screamed from behind me.

I instantaneously dropped to the grass like a sack of potatoes. I landed on my back and looked up at the L.A. Mummy, who was looking down at me, when I saw a flash of silver smash into the L.A. Mummy's face and knock it back on its ass.

Larry had found the glorified butter knife I'd left by the target stand!

"Take *that*, you sick mummy motherfucker!" Larry bellowed.

The knife was dull as a spoon, but the blunt-force trauma still had to hurt like hell.

The small victory was short-lived, however, as the L.A. Mummy bounced to its feet. As it smiled, I noticed it was now missing one of its fangs—good shit, Larry; one down, three more to go.

BANG!

The caustic sound of a gunshot rang through the night.

The L.A. Mummy jumped about three feet into the air and its eyes popped out of its head like a cartoon character. It screeched this awful sound like a pterodactyl getting branded in the ass by a red-hot poker.

"Everyone get the hell down! I ain't fuckin' around here!"

Officer Buscemi.

Larry and I dropped to the ground like a pair of anvils.

I glanced at the L.A. Mummy and it looked… *scared.* Whether it was from the loud noise of the gunshot or the gun itself, I have no idea. It glared at Buscemi for a few moments, its mouth slack in this enormous O, when…

"L.A. MUMMY!"

The L.A. Mummy collapsed to all fours and bestially bounded for the woods like a freaking gazelle.

"HEY! STOP!" Buscemi roared.

Buscemi fired after it—I swear, he must have emptied the whole damn clip—and it even looked like he had gotten a few shots in a leg.

But it didn't matter—the L.A. Mummy didn't slow one iota and disappeared into the dark wilderness, never to be seen again.

I watched its exit until it was gone.

"Man, I fucking hate that guy," I said.

Officer Buscemi holstered his gun and bent to pick up the styrofoam cup of coffee near his feet. Gotta admire a man who places so much stock into their caffeine fix.

He saw Handlebar… or what was left of him anyway.

"Holy *SHIT! Manley!* Officer down… *we've got an officer down!*"

A gaggle of deputies came sprinting over to the corpse.

Buscemi and I locked eyes; he marched to me, fixing me with his classic steely-eyed gaze.

"Kid, I owe you quite the apology."

"You're goddamn right you do!" Larry shouted. "Ya know this *all* could have been avoided, don't ya?! If you dumbasses would have listened to Bark about the freaking mummy, *this never would have—*"

"Larry, that's enough," I said, holding up a hand.

"Yeah, I know," Officer Buscemi replied, looking at his fallen comrade. "I didn't see any green afro or purple pants, but I think I can rightly surmise what that thing was. And that's something I'm gonna have to live with…"

He looked at me.

"I'm sorry, kid. For everything. You were right…
I should have listened."

I couldn't remember the last time I needed a drink
so bad.

I craved it… I *needed* the whiskey burn *now*.

"You alright, kid?"

No.

I did not go to literal Hell and back to relapse and
undo the last three months.

No.

I saw the coffee clutched in Buscemi's hand.

"Steve, hand me that coffee, please," I said.

He looked at me, puzzled.

"I—but kid, my name's not…"

Slowly, his face returned to normal and he handed
me the coffee. I seized it and gulped it all down,
reveling in the magnificent blaze of the hot liquid
sluicing down my throat.

One day at a time.

Fuck you, L.A. Mummy.

A C K N O W L E D G E M E N T S

First and foremost, thank you to my wife for her unwavering commitment to always being my preliminary beta reader and editor. Thank you to my Dad, my Mom, and my two sisters for having always encouraged my overactive and wacky imagination. Thank you to the real-life Bark Mouglas for being such a character as well as the best friend a kooky palooka like myself could ever ask for — love ya, dude. Thank you to my bestie Greg and my crazy cats for forever allowing me to bounce bizarre (and perhaps at times nonsensical) story ideas offa ya. Thank you to Dawn Shea and D&T Publishing for all of your pulchritudinous labors and for taking a chance on this rip-roarin', quirky mummy fable. Thank you to Tom Piccirilli for showing me that it's okay as well as freaking badass to write weird shit, and for making me want to be an author in the first place. Thank you to the Horror Bookstagram community for always providing relentless support. Thank you to all of the marvelous indie horror authors who have gifted me golden nuggets of writing wisdom in addition to being perpetual wellsprings of inspiration.

And thank you, reader. You taking a chance on my Bark-tacular book makes all of this possible.

And worth it.

Thank ya very much.

ABOUT THE AUTHOR

———————┼———————

Whether creating at-home comics or opus-like stories, a lifelong love of all things eldritch and macabre brought Lance to writing. Taking inspiration from daily life and distorting it like a funhouse mirror for your reading enjoyment is what he does best.

Lance lives in a centenarian haunted house in Illinois with his wife and three cats.

He can be found gallivanting Instagram as @Horrorcatlance

ABOUT THE PUBLISHER / EDITOR

Dawn Shea is an author and half of the publishing team over at D&T Publishing. She lives with her family in Mississippi. Always an avid horror lover, she has moved forward with her dreams of writing and publishing those things she loves so much.

Follow her author page on Amazon for all publications she is featured in.

Follow D&T Publishing at their website, **www.dt-publishing.com**, or search for their Facebook Group

Or email here: dandtpublishing20@gmail.com

L.A. Mummy by Lance Loot

Edited by Tasha Schiedel

Cover art by Don Noble

Formatted by Ash Ericmore